Here Comes Rhinoceros

Heinz Janisch · Helga Bansch

Here Comes Rhinoceros

Translated and edited by Evan Jones

Copyright text © 2018 Heinz Janisch
Copyright illustrations © 2018 Helga Bansch
Translated and edited by Evan Jones
Kommt das Nashorn
copyright 2016 by Verlag Jungbrunnen Wein

Published in Canada by Fitzhenry & Whiteside
195 Allstate Parkway, Markham, ON   L3R 4T8
Published in the United States by Fitzhenry & Whiteside
311 Washington Street, Brighton, MA   02135

2 4 6 8 10 9 7 5 3 1
Library and Archives Canada Cataloguing in Publication
Janisch, Heinz
[Kommt das Nashorn. English]
Here comes Rhinoceros / Heinz Janisch ; [illustrated by] Helga
Bansch.

Translation of: Kommt das Nashorn.
ISBN 978-1-55455-448-5 (hardcover)

I. Bansch, Helga, illustrator II. Title. III.Title: Kommt das
Nashorn. English

PZ7.J3675Her 2018   j833'.92   C2018-901711-2

Publisher Cataloging-in-Publication Data (U.S.)

Names: Heinz, Janisch, 1960-, author. | Bansch, Helga, illustrator. | Jones, Evan, 1973-, translator.
Title: Here Comes the Rhinoceros / author, Janisch Heinz ; illustrator, Helga Bansch ; translator, Evan
Jones.
Description: Markham, Ontario : Fitzhenry & Whiteside, 2018. | Originally published in German as:
Kommt Das Nashorn. | Summary: "An illustrated picture book about a rhino, elephant, giraffe, and other
animals that touches on topics of friendship, family, community, nature, commitment and protection" –
Provided by publisher.
Identifiers: ISBN 978-1-55455-448-5 (hardcover)
Subjects: LCSH: Friendship -- Juvenile fiction. | Rhinoceroses -- Juvenile fiction. | Families – Juvenile
fiction. | BISAC: JUVENILE FICTION / Animals / General. | JUVENILE FICTION / Social Themes /
Friendship.
Classification: LCC PZ7.H456He |DDC [E] – dc23

Fitzhenry & Whiteside acknowledges with thanks the Canada Council for the Arts
and the Ontario Arts Council for their support of our publishing program.
We acknowledge the financial support of the Government of Canada through the
Canada Book Fund (CBF) for our publishing activities.

ONTARIO ARTS COUNCIL
CONSEIL DES ARTS DE L'ONTARIO
an Ontario government agency
un organisme du gouvernement de l'Ontario

Canada Council   Conseil des Arts
for the Arts   du Canada

Heinz Janisch · Helga Bansch

Here Comes Rhinoceros

Fitzhenry & Whiteside

Translated and edited by Evan Jones

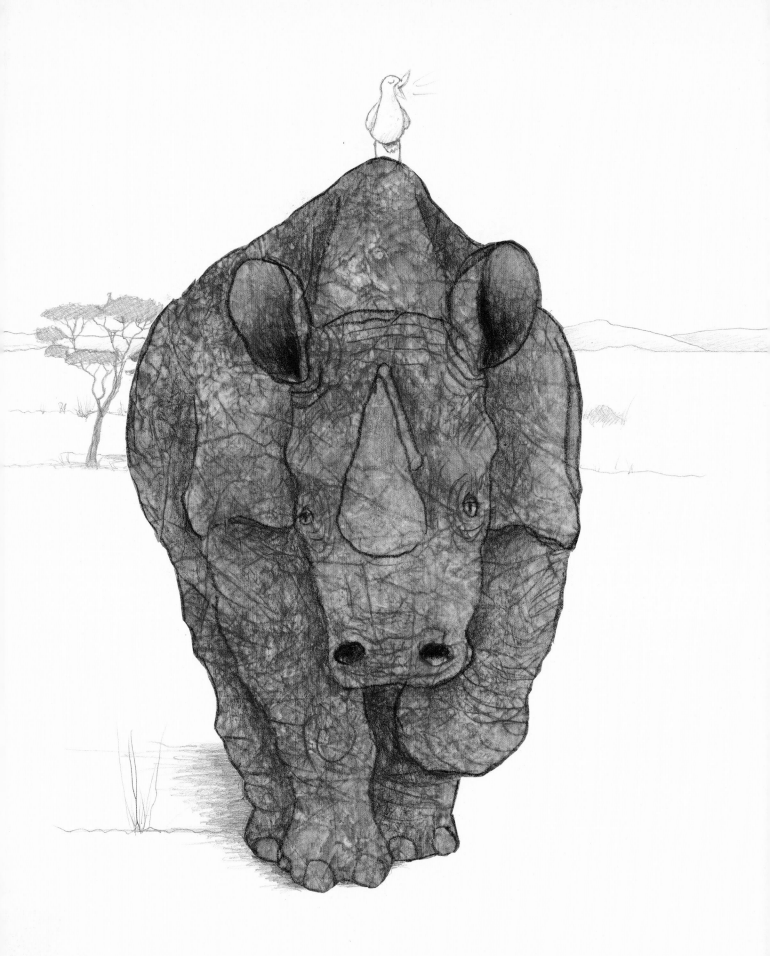

Here comes Rhinoceros.
Beautiful as a mountain.

A tiny bird settles on his back,
gentle as a snowflake,
and chirps.
A tiny bird,
a fellow traveller
who flies away too soon.

Rhinoceros walks on.
The ground trembles,
but the breeze is calm.

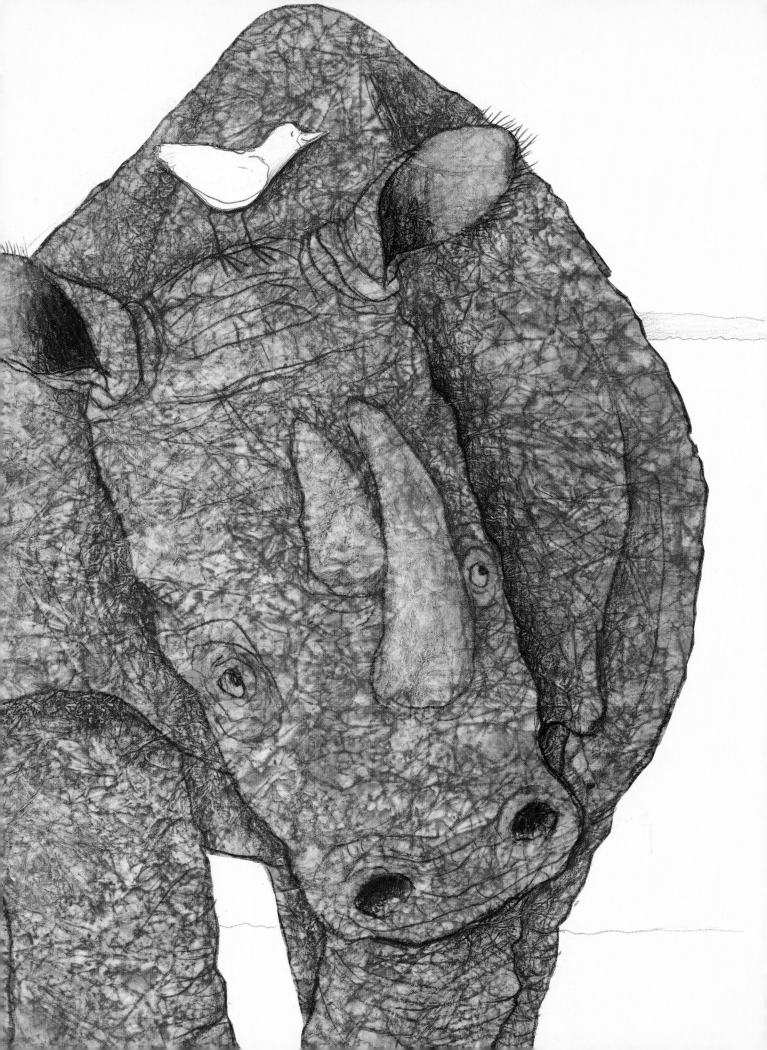

Rhinoceros stops
and looks around.

The animals like him.
They say "Hello."
And "How are you?"
Everyone who passes by does
this.
They come from the sky,
out of the water,
they fly down from above
and pop up from below.

But Rhinoceros is sad.
His horn is crooked.
An accident.

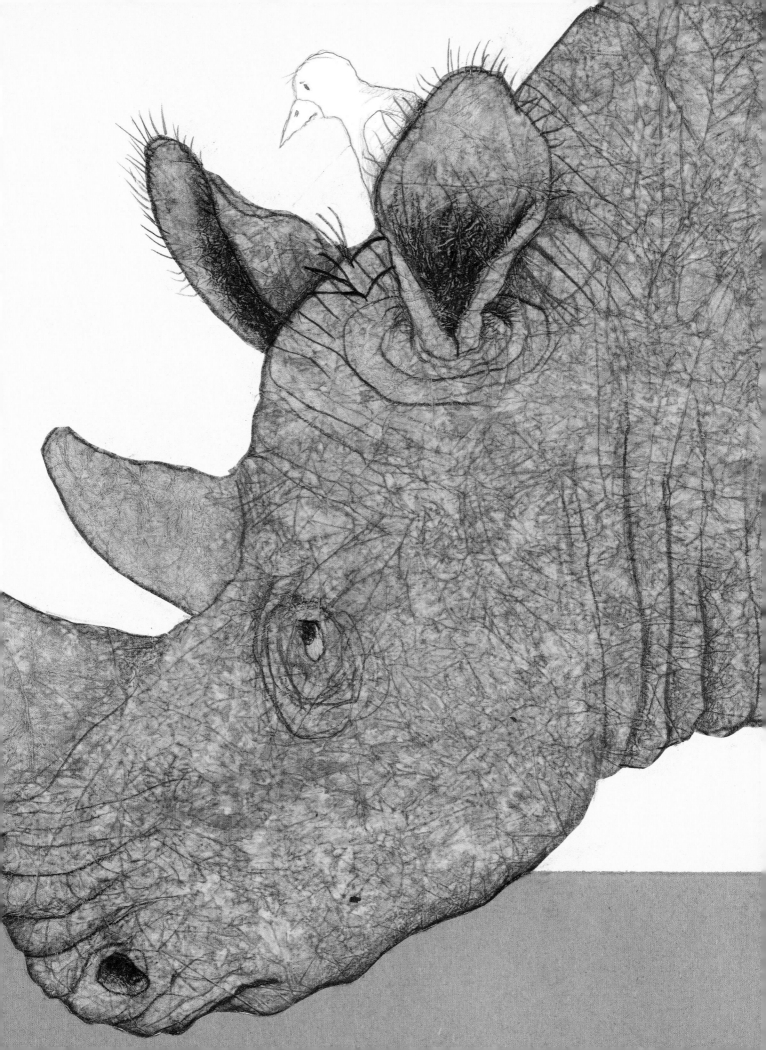

Rhinoceros stops,
holds his ground,
breathes out heavily,
and says, "I wish I was free like that
snowflake."

Rhinoceros
stands there.
Grey as a mountain.

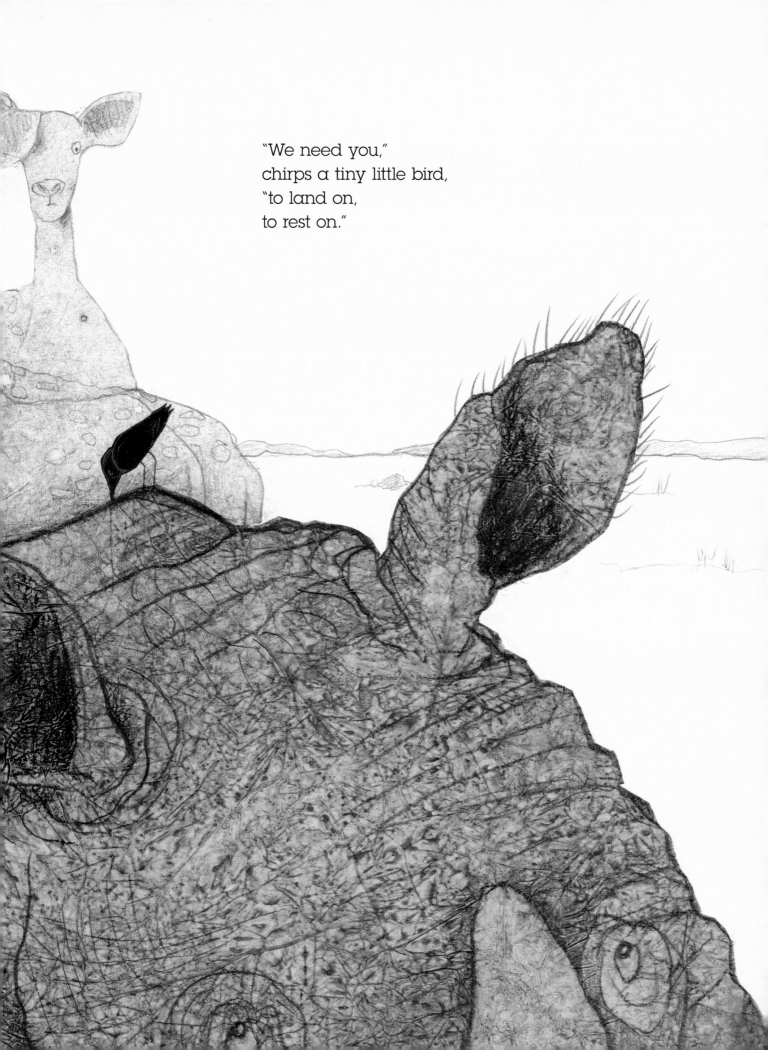

"We need you,"
chirps a tiny little bird,
"to land on,
to rest on."

"You help protect us,"
his friends say as they surround him,
some on top,
some underneath,
some out of the water,
some from the sky.
"As it should be,"
the elephant says.

Here comes Rhinoceros.
Curious as a mountain.
He stands there with his bent horn.
"I wish I were heavy!"
chirps the tiny bird
as the storm blows it off the page.

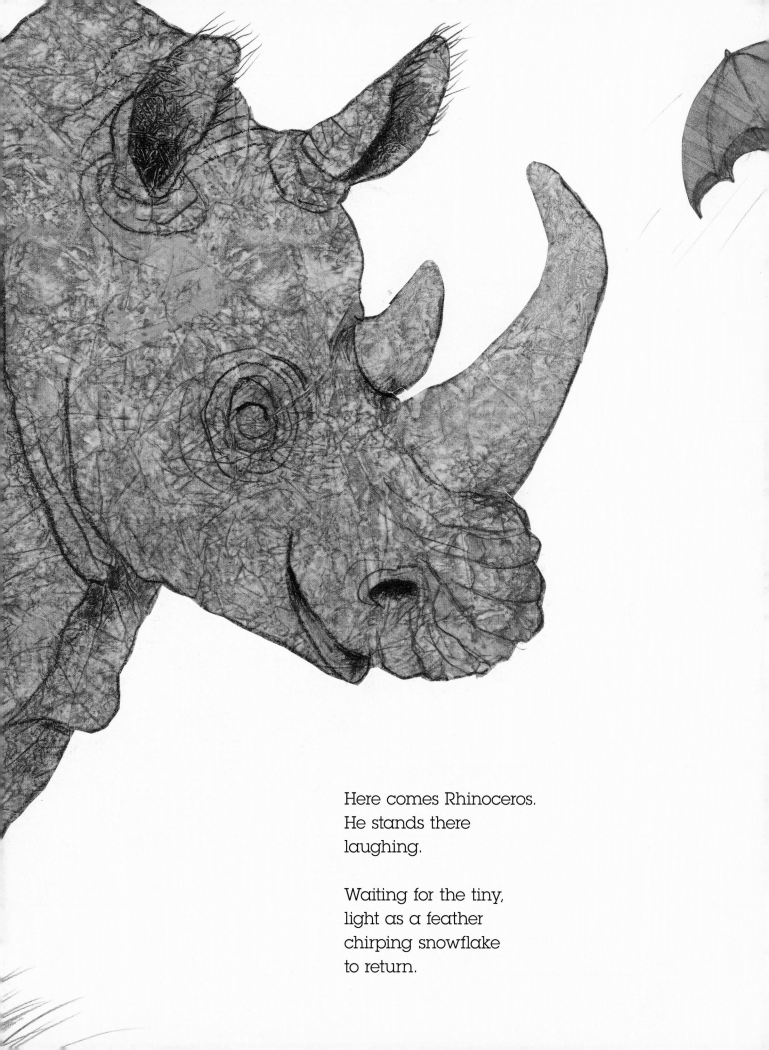

Here comes Rhinoceros.
He stands there
laughing.

Waiting for the tiny,
light as a feather
chirping snowflake
to return.

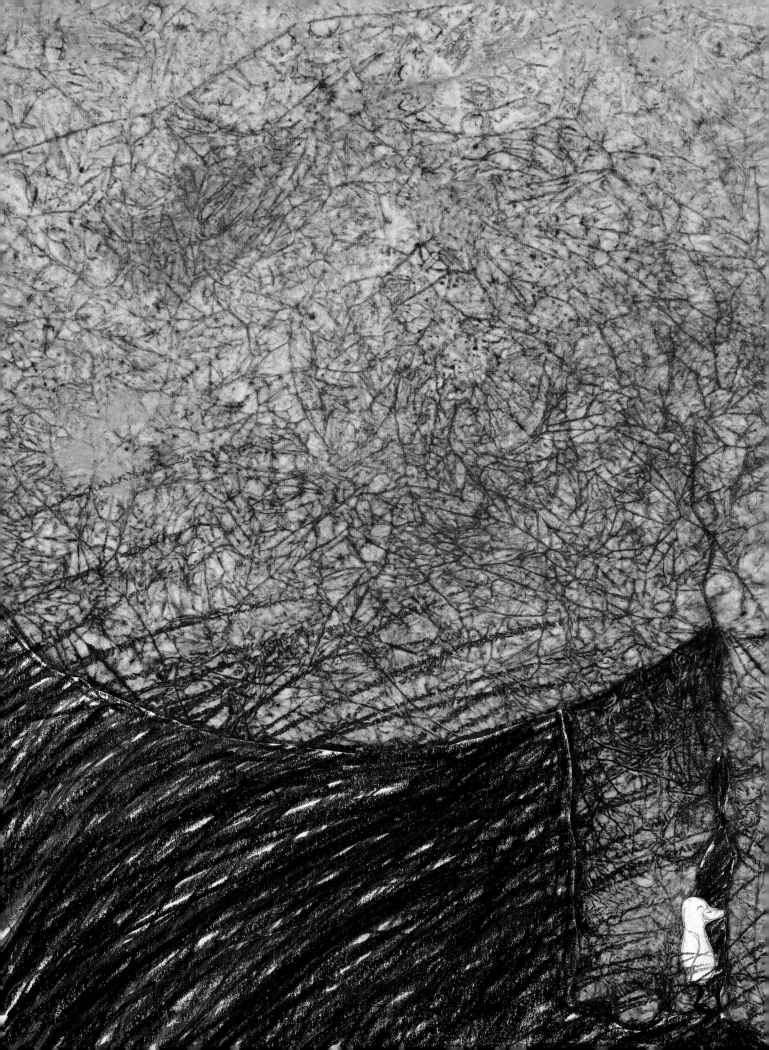

Here comes Rhinoceros.
He stands there,
silent in the storm,
waiting.

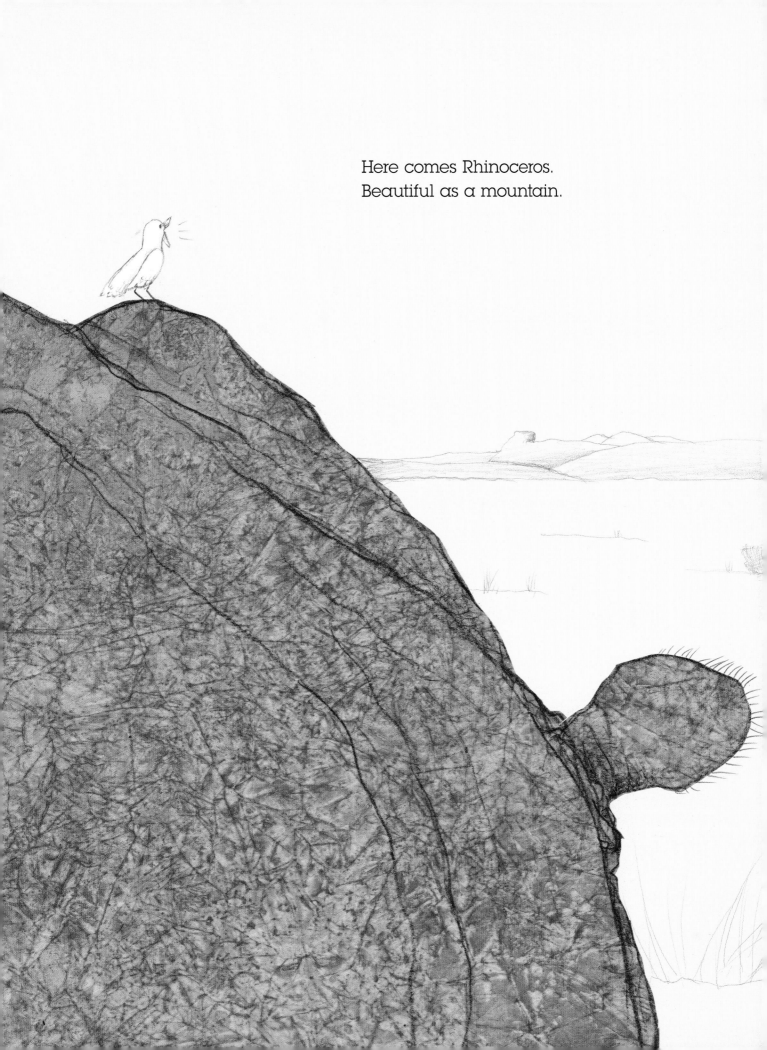

Here comes Rhinoceros.
Beautiful as a mountain.